D1190719

Rixew Awakening

Q. Rosario

ISBN: 978-0-9994200-0-3

Rixew Awakening

Q. Rosario

CONTENTS

Whispers carry in the wind, let the adventure begin…

1 A WARM INTRODUCTION

Stormy nights usually made the wolves feel at ease. But this particular twilight Elvanor Forest was infested with the fierce howls of disgruntled clans. The trees swayed heavily with the wind for miles, moving in chaotic unison within the bounds of the forest. Rain hailed down from the cloudy, grey skies with such force each drop's collision echoed beyond the sound of the next. Lightning and thunder struck one in the same, showing the storm had no intent on giving way.

As the winds continued to batter the trees, their limbs remained intact. The heavy rain turned up the soil. Brush on the forest floor was swept away by turbulent pools of run off rain, zig-zagging through the jagged tree roots that broke the surface. Along the outer limits the forest's greenery was spread thin. Scattered mounds of mud and pools of murky water covered the terrain and the storm continued to regenerate it.

Amongst the rain and the wind, the lightening and the thunder, the wolves danced in the night. The wolves were among the oldest inhabitants of the forest. Their ancestors sprung seven feet tall from between the roots of the first Plenthor Tree. Through the years Elvanor grew, and so did its ecosystem; but the wolves remained among the fiercest and the strongest.

The clans ran, frenzied, along the edges of the forest. Their manes glistened as they danced in the moonlight. Each lightning strike reflected fierce, ravenous images of the monstrous animals. The sharpness of their bone white fangs, curved to the tip, matched that of their black claws. The smallest amongst them stood just over five feet, with a lean and muscular physique. Confidence radiated through their prominent posture. Fore-chest to hind legs they were sculpted and toned through their natural existence.

Violently, the wolves chased at each other, flying through the air kicking up mud and snarling between barks of madness. Others paced circles and incised the trunks of trees, sharpening their deadly claws as they stripped away the bark. Throughout the night more emerged from the depths of the forest. Howls sang out frequently as the wolves called to one another, all but one immersed in the frenzy.

On the very edge of the madness, fur midnight black from tail to muzzle, stood the Rixew. The alpha wolf was over six feet, with his eyes shimmering silver. Still and focused, his fur blew lightly in the wind, the rain dampening its motion just a bit. He stood erect, neck and chest jutting out; and remained motionless while his brethren rallied. Seemingly unaffected by the surrounding chaos, his gaze was fixed in the distance.

His keen sight allowed him to see beyond the vast fields of the stone patched, untamed grasslands and right up to the borders of the Vefren Mountains. Although the storm slightly distorted the scene, the small settlement along the edge of the mountains was as vivid to this beast as it would've been from a few feet away.

At the edge of the mountains, three thatched cottages were arranged in a triangle, with their rears facing the forest. Each had a large barn adjacent to its structure. The green planks making up all the homes were debarked plenthor, and suffered no more than a light shake in the violent winds. A wooden fence, wrapped in razor wire, enclosed the entire rear of the settlement, giving it one large yard. The downpour meshed the crop lines into one mudded pool of soil. In its entirety the settlement was no more than three hundred square feet. The houses were nearly seventy feet apart with the fence connected around the two furthest from each other.

In the dark of the night, the rear showed no sign of activity. A single candlelit lantern swung from the doorknob of the rightmost house, where the gate ended. Its barn sat closest to the narrow road that curved out of mountains just three hundred yards away. There, is where the humbled wolf's eyes were locked.

A small gap in the mountain chain made the road identifiable from a distance in the storm. It appeared darker than the night and even in the day its abrupt curve would've made it impossible to view the channel past a few yards.

As the storm continued its onslaught, the rain did not let up. Rounds of thunder were accompanied by the maniac snarls of the wolf clans. Yet, the Rixew remained calm when he caught the first glimpse of light creep into the mountain path. A silhouette followed within seconds of the light, turning the corner and coming into full view. The person's attire was obscured by the darkness, but the sword protruding from his hip, along with the banner pole in his hand, made it evident he was a soldier.

Following the first figure, a troupe of dressed soldiers three wide in rank emerged from the mountain path. All were adorned in metal armor. Two outside men brandished torches every four rows. As the light illuminated the distant scene the wolves began to calm themselves. Their banter shifted to attentiveness, accompanied by viscous growls. They were nearly as still and focused as their leader while they waited. The last set of men to emerge from the mountain made it a company of thirty-seven soldiers, with the commander leading the way.

Lights flickered on in the first and second homes, as the front of the troupe was nearly upon the first cottage. The Rixew tilted his head back, as if he were addressing the storm itself, and let out the fiercest howl heard in the night. With instant aggression the wolves took off. Covering yards of terrain in single leaps, hurtling mud and loose debris to the rear of the drive, they were in unison and ready for action.

The Rixew's eyes housed his aggression as he led the pack with unnatural discipline. Howls from the clans strengthened his stride and his gaze grew in intensity as he neared the dwelling. The wolves were a few yards from the gate before soldiers noticed them. They were just upon the first cottage when a few motioned at the growing closeness of the barks coming from the direction of the forest. Forced upon their wits the solders did not falter, nor break ranks.

"Three at each! Drag them from their homes! The rest with me!" the captain at the head of the company screamed.

Six solders immediately broke ranks making way to the cottages. The captain turned his attention to the oncoming hoard. When the wolves were seconds away from jumping the fence, a silent motion from the alpha's tail sent him half racing to the far side of the settlement as he leapt. Their swiftness and agility sent shocks of horror through the soldiers watching. With half the pack obscured from his vision, the captain motioned for a few of his order to break to avoid being flanked. As the wolves came closer, the soldiers took their defensive positions. Balance was difficult on the murky terrain. Constantly they were brushing rainwater from their hardened faces. They drew their swords and mounted their shields. Nature was against them.

With a final howl the Rixew took a twenty-foot leap, eliminating the remaining distance between him and the nearest soldiers. Clearing the captain completely, he landed, muzzle wide open, on the helm of the soldier directly behind him. Unable to fling his arms in defense, the man dropped his sword and staggered. The wolf tore his helmet off with ease and snapped onto the back of the soldier's neck, ripping it from the man's body with a single jerk. First blood was drawn as they headed to the ground. Soldiers nearby hardly wiped the splatters from their faces and readied to retaliate before the rest of the wolves were amongst them.

The captain made no effort to turn around and see the man's dying efforts. As quickly as the first soldier was over his head another was at his feet. He plunged his sword toward the wolf's back, catching mud as it veered to the right then leaped to snap at the place where the man's face had been. Swinging around with his full might he hit the animal's hind leg with the edge of his sword. Howls of pain were accompanied by screams of agony before a stab between its eyes hurried the crippled animal's death.

The wolves were overtook the group in seconds. Men lucky enough to evade or eliminate a threat only found himself ready to face another. As quickly as the Rixew killed the first man he leapt to a second. A few of his hoard were slain before he was at the throat of a third, and the man's reaction was too quick for him to catch him clean. He grabbed the wolf by his upper and lower jaw in midair, wincing at the pain in his pierced fingers as he attempted to tear them apart. With his foreleg, the Rixew slashed the man across the face releasing himself. Just as the soldier went to clasp the gash at the corner of his right eye, the animal grabbed his hand and ripped it off with a single thrust.

The man's scream echoed against the howls and thunder. Dropping to his knees, he leaned his face into the heart of the wolf's chest. Matted fur sunk into his eyes. Slow breaths escaped the wolf's lungs; his chest rising and falling with each. The air escaping through his nose was vivid in the cold of the storm. Curses of men and wolves alike filled the air, as he surveyed the scene.

Before the Rixew could finish off the soldier his attention was drawn to a nearby house. Leaping over the broken soldier, allowing him to fall face first into the mud gripping his severed limb, the Rixew raced toward the dirt road spanning the front of the cottages. From the far end he could tell a few of his kin were slain but less than a handful off soldiers remained.

The front door on the far cottage was ajar and loose on its hinge, but the house was absent of activity other than the fighting in front. Shadows danced around the windows of the middle house. The soldiers shut the door after they had entered to prevent any wolves from following them. The cottage closest to the mountain path was completely ablaze. After forcefully taking the occupants from their home, the soldiers set it on fire.

Flames engulfed the house as an elder man knelt weeping curses in front. He was soaked, heaving hard against the smoke polluting the air. Behind him a young boy was holding his ground against a solider, fending off the armored man's blows with the thick off a branch. Standing just over five and a half feet Sailen Ortow's strength was wearing thin. His defensive was growing weak under the might of the soldier and his sword.

Staggering with the last of his breath, he exclaimed, "So, this is the King's will?" Weariness forced his demand for reprieve to a mere panting whimper. "You are here; you see our barren fields, no more than dirt. Yet you still ravage our homes and shed blood in the name of empire tax?"

The soldier was silent. Removing his metal helmet, he cleared the mud and sweat from his eyes, smirking as he gripped his sword with both hands. As he tightened his single embrace around the branch, the boy could tell it would not withstand another blow.

"I hope your wages are enough to clear your conscience."

Gathering the last of his strength he lifted the branch just as the soldier heaved his sword to the sky. The sword came whistling through the air, but before it met its victim the Rixew slammed its body against the soldier. The great wolf's fangs were fully planted in the side of the man's face, crushing it. The man's body shook wildly on the ground. Blood burst from the tears in his flesh, covering his entire right side in red as he seized, making quakes in the mud mounds and pools beneath him.

Astonished, and immediately realizing the luck of his fate, the boy turned and ran to his father, still weeping in front of the house, before the wolf pulled himself from the scene.

"Father we must go, we must go! They will kill us!" Dropping his wooden club, he threw himself beneath the man's shoulder and attempted to lift him, but fell to the ground underneath the dead weight. "This is no time for self-pity, we must go."

His second attempt to lift his absent-minded father ended when he heard rabid snarls at his back. He could feel the warm, slow breaths down the nape of his neck. The distant screams and barks accompanying the storm around him were suddenly void. Slowly he moved from underneath his father. Slower still he turned and eased himself up, his face inches from the underside of the black wolf's snout.

Blood dripped onto him from the muzzle of the

Rixew, his gazed affixed upward on the silver eyes of the wolf. He was completely mesmerized in the presence of the great wolf. As if by magic, all his fatigue vanished. The aches in his bones dulled and he slowly stood upright. The urgent need for survival forced attentiveness; his mind started thinking of every logical ploy to escape his present danger.

"I. mean you no harm," the boy started, his tone was steadier than anticipated. Calmly he held the wolf's gaze, trying not to come across as a threat or defenseless prey. The Rixew breathed slowly, tail stiff and intent in expression. The surrounding events slowly started to become clear to the boy's senses again, and panic caused him to search for a way out.

Unwilling to make any sudden moves, his vision became completely distorted as the rainwater clouded his sight. He could feel the heaviness of his soaked clothing and the surrounding sounds of madness. Blinking hard in hopes to clear his line of sight, he took a light step back, immediately sparking a snarl from the wolf.

"Please, I know you understand me..." he began, but was immediately distracted by slams and screams escaping from the neighboring house. Disregarding circumstance; turning to the direction of the commotion he caught sight of a soldiers dragging a young girl and small boy, out of the home kicking and screaming.

"No!" Fumbling to his, knees he began searching for his club, cautiously side-eyeing the giant wolf. The Rixew took off before he was back on his feet. Making his way to rescue the pair, the boy watched as the soldier dropped the two screaming children and struggled to draw his blade to combat the Rixew who was rabidly making its way to him.

Just as the wolf closed in another soldier ran from the house, sword in the air ready to help his comrade. He spanned the three steps in front of the cottage in one jump, swinging his sword and narrowly missing the Rixew's tail as he passed the spot. The wolf's precision once again surpassed expectations. His jaw caught and crushed the chain mail surrounding the soldier's neck. The man met the ground, kicking and whaling for relief, to no end.

Thinking fast, the Sailen hurled his club with all his might at the remaining soldier who was attempting to slay the Rixew from behind. "Meerah, move!" The girl grabbed her brother and jumped out of the way just as the stick hit the soldier's head, knocking off his helm. Dropping his sword, the soldier staggered forward trying to gain his balance and slipped in the wet soil. Sailen recovered the dropped sword and raised it. Crashing on all fours just a few feet away from his cohort's convulsing corpse, the soldier was trapped between a ravage clan of wolves and the tip of the sword, now in the boy's hands.

Surveying the remains of his home, Sailen gripped his sword tighter. He watched the few remaining soldiers escape onto the mountain path with their lives, wolves howling at their heels. The heat from his blazing home a few yards away passed in waves over his face. His father, now having gathered himself, and neighbors were looking to him for signs of action.

"So...," the soldier began in an overly confident, deep voice, with his back to Sailen. "Will you give me a quick, honorable death... or leave me to the beasts?" The man's voice was relaxed, accompanied by a rash chuckle that made it seem like he welcomed death with confidence.

Sailen's eyes were locked with the Rixew. He was now standing over his latest triumph, muzzle still dripping blood. Mud tracks and blooded bodies laced the land. With the storm in full swing, lightening illuminated the surviving wolves' wild, blood-thirsty appearance.

Meerah Lowti held her weeping baby brother tight just feet away from the center scene, eyeing the savage wolves in horrific wonder. The hopeless soldier peered up at the wolf's underside waiting for the slightest sign of movement. "Tell me, is there honor in your business here?" Sailen appeared to speak with wisdom beyond his years. Shocked, the soldier hesitated.

"I am but a carrier of actions for a higher order, I bear no business of my own." With these last words the soldier swiveled and kicked Sailen at the ankles causing him to fall and drop the sword. Catching the blade of the sword with both hands, the soldier swung it around just in time to strike the attacking Rixew in the foreleg with enough force to send him falling into the mud. Mad barks escaped from the wolf as he slid.

The man turned to Sailen, flipping the sword in the air to grasp the hilt. As he strode, howls echoed louder than storm. Sailen fumbled back toward the cottage behind him, peering past the forthcoming soldier who was oblivious to the horde of wolves nearly upon him. It was as if he thought his death would be righteous in merit as long as the boy's life was taken.

In an instant, a wolf, bloodied in his eyes, had its mouth around the soldier's thigh. Pain slowed his reaction.

Before he was able let out a scream, another wolf was on his shoulder, claws sunk past the metal on his chest and into his flesh. At the time the last one jumped on his back and teared, screams of agony escaped the helpless man. He was ravaged alive. His body flared in desperation as more wolves joined the attack.

Sailen regained his senses and hurried to force Meereah and her brother back up the steps and into their cottage. He turned for his father Bell, almost forgetting him. But, Bell was managing to force himself in their direction.

Sailen realized they were fortunate to make it into the house. He slammed the wooden door and slid to the floor with his back pressed hard against it, listening to the screams of the last soldiers. Moans escaped the dead and dying as the night was left to the storm. Howls became the only sounds prominent amidst the thunder. Feeling a body lightly press against him in the dark, Sailen put his arm around Osem, Meerah's little brother, and remained still.

2 HUMBLING TASKS

"Sailen...Sailen..." Meerah shook Sailen's shoulders, trying to wake him. He was sleeping against the cottage door. Slowly lifting his head, weariness evident in his face, he rubbed his eyes to wake and clear his vision. Osem began to stir at his side, a bit more energetic.

"Meerah?" Sailen hesitated as he made his way upright, Osem easing off of him. Natural light beamed into the cottage room from the morning sun, highlighting areas of the room and emphasizing the dust and dirt matted to the windows.

Barely able to stretch his worn body, Sailen got to his feet and looked around the Meerah's house. The living room contained very little furniture and was draped with woven tapestries that covered parts of the walls and floors. His dad was resting near an overturned wooden chair by the fireplace in a deep sleep, with his back to the three of them. Sailen knew the kitchen was behind the interior wall of the room and that the stairs near the door led to the bedrooms on the upper floor.

"Where are your parents?" Sailen asked Meerah without making eye contact.

She was now sitting on the bottommost step that led to the second floor, near the door. Osem remained on the floor near the door. He was silent, but content. The morning sunlight was shining through the windows, highlighting the innocence in his youthful face. He had deep brown eyes and hardly a blemish on his fair skin. He had only recently turned three and didn't know all that was happening. Meerah picked her head up from between her arms, most of the color drained from her lightly freckled cheeks, caramel and rose from irritation. Slowly, her eyes, the same deep brown as her brothers, met Sailen's and he could see her tears building up.

"They were killed..." she began, "Father heard the soldiers marching from the Vefren path, but couldn't get us to the cellar quick enough." She paused and gazed out the window at the front of the house. Following her, Sailen's eyes fell upon the portion of the night's massacre visible through the windowpane.

Carnage crowded the settlement; carcasses of soldiers and wolves were littered across the ground. Sailen turned to Osem, "Are you still sleepy pal?" Osem replied with a silent nod.

"Go over there and rest by my father, Meerah and I are going to step outside for a bit."

Osem got up and made his way towards Bell by the fireplace. After setting the wooden chair up right, without stirring the old man, he climbed into it and balled up into a comfortable resting position.

Meerah got up and made her way toward the door. Sailen opened it, contemplating how to delay the torment of locating Meerah's parents. Covering his eyes with his free arm, he stepped outside. The sky was clear. Sunlight shown straight down onto the house; by its location Sailen could tell it was fairly early in the day.

Chirps escaped birds and critters puttering throughout the settlement and along the mountain border. There was a light breeze. The surrounding greenery swayed gently. All of nature but the ground itself escaped the ominous glow of misery. Head tilted to the sky, Sailen motioned Meerah toward him. "It's clear now, but late afternoon will bring sky predators." She preceded him off the porch, knowing exactly what he meant.

Carcasses were scattered all across the dwelling, to the opening at the base of the Vefren Mountains. Blood pools clotted dirt patches where the ground was still moist. Partly severed limbs hung by threads, while others rested near the edge of bloodied blades or in the maw of a wolf. The ghastly expressions of those fortunate enough to have died without their face in the ground reflected the chaos of the night's events.

Amidst the homestead, Meerah's house was the only one left standing. The two houses on either side of hers were burned to their foundations. A few wooden structural members protruded through each, but all levels were completely gone. Sailen looked across the dismal scene, an ambiguous expression hiding his emotions.

"I don't understand," Meerah said looking back to the porch, knowing neither of them could answer. At fifteen,

Sailen was only a year younger than Meerah, matching her in height, but with a more muscular build do to their farm labor lifestyle. In deep visual investigation of his blooded appearance, he stepped off the porch and slowly strode towards her, brushing dirt and filth from his tattered clothes.

"For one reason or another..." he began, as he stepped past her, "we have attracted the King's hostile attention." His words reflected further action over observation. Meerah could sense the growing animosity and aggression swelling in him, not new, but emotions prior helpless and void of life.

Growing up, they were the subjects of exploitation by the empire's invisible hand. The Hulren King claimed rights to all in the realm of Yelerah, the known Land of Life. All residents were under his control and subject to excessive abuse. They have silently resented this since the land's inception. "The wolves... they..." Meerah cut herself off. , she knew neither she nor Sailen could began to speculate on their presence. Minutes passed and the silence seemed awkwardly comforting as they took it in, hardly scathed by the gruesomeness of everything by now, unnatural for their ages. "We should bury the bodies before they're ravaged by predators, it'll take a day's labor."

Without completely turning to her, "No, that would honorable, they've earned no honor." Meerah stared at him with admiration and worry. This brash dishonor of the dead was unheard of. "We'll strip them of their armor and let their bodies fertilize the land." Taking a few steps forward he turned to her, "Then we leave before dark."

"Leave?'" she asked, searching his eyes for more.

"We can't stay here, that number of soldiers being sent out into a less than village from the Empire is unheard of. They came here with purpose, and whether they achieved it or not, I'm sure more will be back to confirm or rectify. We shall make for Orium. There we can try contact Plruip." Reading her mind he added, "and hope we don't run into any of those wolves on our way there."

He shifted his gaze to one of the dead wolves less than 5 yards away, just as beautiful and menacing in death as it was in life. Its half open mouth showed its bone white fangs, their sharp curve naturally dripped clean of blood and gore. With its eyes closed, the grey wolf appeared to be in a deep slumber, its size and ferocious beauty preserved in splendor. Envy crept over Salein's. Everything about this animal he wanted himself, for all it would give him; grace, beauty, strength, power, admiration, even the aura of the highest royalty. He'd never seen these wolves in his all his life and though he was terrified of them in every way imaginable, he hoped it wouldn't be the last.

Bell took Osem just past the Vefren path, outside the settlement. They harvested Teetle berries from the bushes bordering the mountains while Meerah and Sailen cleared the homestead. The berries were a bright aqua, and stood out against the deep green shrubbery they sprouted on. Osem plucked them from the bushes and laughed as he squashed them in his hand, staining his fingertips and smearing it across his palms. He loved it. Bell smiled as he watched Osem's self-induced pleasure. He filled his burlap sack with the berries and strained to focus his thoughts on something.

The Teetle berries had been a major staple in their

diet since they'd lived along the edge of the mountains; they were eaten for nourishment, and used along with herbs native to the area for minor illness remedies that didn't need major medical attention. Getting medical attention would require them to make the day's trip to Orium. It was avoided if possible. Bell ate a handful, then continued gathering, thoughts muddled and lightly pleasured.

Clearing the soldiers bodies was stomach churning. Saile and Meerah spent the day stripping them of armor and dragging them to the rear of the settlement. It was gruesome and it only seemed to get worse as they went on.

The soldiers' armor was easy enough to remove. It was made from heavy, resistive steel, but designed for functionality as well as protection, making it easy for them to attack as well as defend. They could dress and undress with ease. The armor was decorated and fashioned with intricate attention to detail. Every uniform engraved with scripted initials, gold clad trim, and as bright as a mirror's reflection where not stained with blood and grime. Occasionally a curiosity distracted them from the horrifying part of their labors, but more often than not they were repulsed by the condition of the corpses.

Each soldier's helm was removed first as it was the easiest to do. For all the detail in the uniform's design, simple clasps held each soldier's front side armor to its back. They unclasped the breast and back plates from both sides, unshackled the steel plated over their boots, and did the same for the armor along the lower body. Heavy as it was, removing the armor was only a fraction of the struggle. Varying degrees of bodily mutilation made stripping every soldier a revolting puzzle. By the third one,

Sailen and Meerah had completely given up on caution and resolved to move through it quickly. They dragged each body to the back of the settlement and packed all the metal armor in the remains of Sailen's backhouse.

Grief wore over both of them. It took just over three hours to strip and relocate all of the soldiers. The physical exhaustion and the stench of the bodies wore on them heavily. Although they stomached the ordeal, the appearance of so much torn human flesh, ripped cartilage and broken bones disgusted them immensely. Many of the soldiers had their throats ripped clean out. Tubes and innards remained where skin flapped open. Other bodies had gruesome bites and claw tears over their faces and bodies, deep puncture wounds that caused them to bleed to death. If Sailen and Meerah weren't accustomed to butchering their own livestock, they probably wouldn't have been able to stomach the task.

The sun was making its way across the sky. It was almost noon, and within a few hours, lured in by the scent of blood and flesh, sky predators would arrive. Time was of the essence, and it also wasn't. They had no crops to harvest, no fields to till, but they had to get to Orium, sooner than later and that was a journey of its own.

"We should take as much as we can carry with us for trade," Sailen stated, sitting on a stump just outside the open barn.

"Don't you think people will be suspicious? It won't be easy to trade off. And if we run into any soldiers, we're as good as dead in the capital dungeon." Meerah responded.

"It's a chance," Sailen replied. "We have nothing

else. We can leave most of it on the edge of the city and see how we make out with a few pieces. Let's hope my dad knows a few people in Orium dealing black market goods."

"Let us hope..." Meerah replied, staring off toward the Vefren Path.

Sailen surveyed what remained of the settlement. He knew it wasn't likely they'd ever return, and he felt strangely comfortable with that. "Grab my dad and pack what food you can. I'm going to look through the armor and see what's worth taking." Dusting off her stained blouse, Meerah got up from the stump and started toward Bell and Osem.

Sailen got up from the stoop. "In two hours we'll head out to make camp a little way Vefren Path, it'll be safer being in the mountains than here."

"Let us hope." Forcing a smile, she walked off.

Two hours was just enough time for Sailen. He located Meerah's parents', Rinah and Hittra Lowti, bodies, dug graves as deep as he could in his exhausted state, and then buried them fast so Meerah and Osem wouldn't have to see the bodies. The violence of their deaths showed no mercy. It was horrible for him to have to bury his neighbors in such a state; they were family to him. It would've been unbearable for Meerah.

After searching the remains of the third house, Sailen could find no trace of Yuefil Ondagger. Doubting her ability to have escaped, he assumed the elderly woman was taken. Thus, the grave he initially dug for her body remained empty.

Once he was done, Sailen gathered everyone. No words were shared over the graves. They stood in silence,

Osem wrapped around his sister's legs mixed in emotions. Meerah's tears were silent and painful. They were strong people, but agony tore at her insides. Sailen and Bell were also plagued with pain and grief.

Bell pulled Meerah in his arms. "It will be all right child," he said softly, knowing there was no comfort in his empty words. He gently stroked her hair, as she wept harder. Recognizing his sister's emotions, Osem began to cry. Sailen fought his urge and put his watchful eyes to the sky.

3 SUBTLE ENCOUNTERS

Midday had come and gone, the sun was setting. Ease was over the day, but horror lingered. The sun cooked the naked corpses littered along the back of the homestead. The pungent, foul odor could be picked up from a great distance. Small animals and critters returned to their dwellings; the valley was now void of life. The company of four was on the edge of the village, at the crack of the Vefren path.

Sailen fumbled with the burden of the armor and food, trying to organize it comfortably for their journey. Although it wasn't a lot, between them all they carried three suits of armor, with two extra helmets and breastplates. The bulk proved tough to manage along with the food rations they brought. Bell carried an armor set and hefty portion of the food in a burlap shoulder sling. Sailen wore a breastplate and had the other two sets of armor tightly packed on his back with a shield covering them. On his waist he carried a sword, and sheathed a small knife in his right boot. They all packed blades for protection on the road, except Osem. Meerah hoisted food in a shoulder sling while wearing a breastplate, knowing she'd have to keep a hand on Osem. The boy was left carrying a single helm, mostly because he fussed, feeling left out not carrying anything.

"Did we leave anything?" Bell laughed, getting a cheerful response from Osem.

"Nothing worth bringing..." Meerah replied, reaching out to grab Osem's hand. As she peered back to get a final look of their destroyed home, she glimpsed dark shadows beginning to stretch across the sky from Elvanor Forest. The shadows, they'd only seen once before,

The shadows were moving across the sky quickly. Bell was the first to communicate the exigency of their situation, forcing everyone forward. They rushed into the Vefren path, Meerah picking up Osem to get along faster. Rushing to make it to the first crook of the path. Bell grabbed Osem from Meerah, giving her a better chance at getting on. Osem was unaware of what was happening, but sensing the alarm, he began to get a frantic in Bell's arms. As they advanced on to the first crook, Sailen looked back saw the shadows now completely covered their home. Unable to look away, he quickly turned the crook bumping into Meerah, causing them both to stumble a few steps before catching their balance.

Sailen helped Meerah up and dusted her off before himself. "Sorry about that..." he offered.

"You've done worse," she snickered in reply.

"The soldiers that fled last night may not be that far

ahead of us. It's getting dark and I think we should make way off the path for a while and set up camp."

"Higher ground of course," Bell answered.

In the shadows of the mountains, nature had taken them in, between the mass of the natural ridges and growth. At the beginning, the Vefren path was made of stone and mostly free of brush. Small trees and bushes were scattered along the mountainside. Further up the path, the mountain became more wooded until it was completely consumed for hundreds of miles before the outlet: Orium to the north and the village of Keentha to the east.

They walked up the side of the mountain looking for a suitable resting spot. Osem still a bit shaken, while clinging to Meerah and constantly whined for his parents. By nightfall they were nearly three miles from the start of crook.

They laid off on a stone patch a quarter mile up the mountain from the path. Three trees sheltered the patch from the back, while the front was open but spanned jagged rock and dirt patches.

Sailn, Meerah and Bell unloaded their packs. Meerah took three blankets from her pack and gave one each to Bell and Sailen. She handed out Teetle berries and bread, unpacked a flask they would all drink from. They would go without fire or hot food for the night. Such a precaution was necessary since they didn't know how close any of the fleeing soldiers were. But there was very little happening on this part of the mountain.

The night was dark, but as their eyes adjusted they were able to see a good distance.

With a sudden discomfort, Sailen noticed two sets

of eyes watching him intensely from the brush just off the campsite. They were exceptionally sharp and piercing, he was amazed that no one else noticed. The eyes were clearly locked on him, as if they were peering into his soul. Both pairs were a deep green surrounded by vivid white. From the size of them, he assumed they belonged to a feral animal or a large owl. He could not make out the figures, but in an effort not to panic the others he didn't observe them for too long.

After a few minutes they disappeared with a single blink, off to join the happenings of the night. *"Owls usually don't hunt in pairs,"* he thought to himself.

Osem was amazed by the night on the mountain. He pointed out every star in the sky to his sister, and she happily engaged his amusement. It was their first night away from home. The serenity and mystery of nature both excited and frightened them. They sat and silently observed, and ate enough to hold off their hunger.

Bell motioned for them to come in closer, and broke the silence. "Tomorrow will be more dangerous. We will have to watch for predators, as well as sink holes and terrain channels. The path has taken many people over time. Some fall victim to the elements, others get lost, and even more become prey for vexers or mountain lions.

"It's been a while since I've been to Orium but I have a friend, Elogh Kilont, who may take us in… if we get rid of this this armor first… " he hesitated. "He won't want money or trade, but he also won't want any trouble with the capital. Elogh has enough troubles of his own." Bell then spread out and laid flat on his back, looking at the sky. Taking his cue, they all did the same. Osem cuddled against

Meerah as they all stared into the night, weary and afraid.

Sailen remembered hearing the name Elogh before. He recalled the story his father once told him about his friend; one of the many tall tales Sailen once thought misadventure and mischief. His father loved to mix his life adventures in with Sailen's bedtime stories. The mention of lifesaving Elogh hiding Bell from soldiers who were looking to imprison him for possessing a black market a sheath he'd found. There was much excitement to the story, and Sailen felt respect for the man for helping his father.

As he lay there his mind wandered to his own adventures and current predicament, but more specifically the Rixew. Why were the wolves at his homestead and where had they come from? Sailen could hear Meerah weeping throughout the night, and telling Osem how much she loved him and that everything was going to be ok. Her heart was broken and her life was taken from her, but he knew her spirit was still intact. Losing her parents was an emotional disruption, but she'd bounce back in time.

He began to feel his own distress. He had lost his home, and although his life up until now had been all about finding a way out of the mundane, now he felt bitter remorse. Knowing he'd lost a big part of himself along with a home and family. He felt rage.

With little undisturbed sleep through the night, Sailen was up just before the sun. He wandered around the mountain, not too far out of sight from their spot, taking advantage of the time to himself. The sun would be up in minutes, and though they were still in the shadow of the mountain, it would make the day a little brighter. There wasn't much life where they were, and no sign of the piercing green eyes that had spooked him the night before. After making sure the camp area was mostly safe, he wandered off to scout the mountain path.

Near thirty feet from the path he began to hear voices speaking. Unsheathing his blade, he knelt down to avoid being seen. He strained his ear to listen and attempted to detect what direction the voices were going. Hearing a gallop and knew they were on horseback. This meant they were headed towards his village. The soldiers that arrived the previous night were not on horseback. Was this a follow up troupe sent to scout the scene and make sure the job was done? Were they sent to ensure there were no survivors?

A series of rock arrangements hid Sailen from view. He could hear the slow trot of the horses. He peeked up to get a quick look, not realizing the path was in line with the soldiers, now no more than a few feet away. He'd been spotted immediately and there was no sense in ducking back down.

Three men on horseback were now headed toward him. Spotting him, they kicked their heels and advanced. With a rush of adrenaline and instinct, Sailen jumped up, blade in hand. He had slept in one of the breastplates he carried, but other than that the men were armed much better than he was. Untrained and outnumbered, he only hoped to lead them away from the others, then figure out an escape afterwards.

In the area the Vefren Path was pretty narrow, and the men could attack him no more than two at a time. They spoke no words, honed their weapons and charged at Sailen. He ran between the first two slicing one's hand as the man tried to grab for him. Both screamed in anger. Their attempts to turn their horses around to chase after him were poorly executed, causing one to tumble and become trapped under his flailing horse. With the remaining two still on horseback, Sailen stood braced in place.

Within ten feet of them, they each came to a halt, laughing harshly at his immobilized state. Sailen knew there was no way out.

"So…what will it be..." Sailen stated, not showing any sign of distress.

"I didn't realize we gave you permission to inquire," the man facing Sailen answered. "But none the less, you obviously are at our disposal at the moment... so…" The soldier came off his horse and started petting near its mouth. He paid no attention to his strugglinh comrade.

Sailen noticed that the man was not as clean and well-kept as he'd thought men of this stature would be, assuming he was a soldier. The man had dirt around his face and his hair was unkempt. Sailen tried not to let his mind ponder who or what they were, and instead focused on his current predicament.

He could sense the man not moving behind him, but his presence was still there. The other man who had fallen off his horse was struggling to regain composure, wincing and cursing his sliced hand. "Kill this peasant boy Milfor! Or I'll make easy work of him," he screamed.

"Mind yourself," Milfor, replied. "You let this untrained 'peasant' best you." He spoke with mocking disdain. Directly to Sailen he asked, "What brings you into the mountain?"

The disgruntled man was not pleased by his

embarrassment, or the courtesy his leader was extending to this boy. Sailen, unshaken, continued to look the man in front of him in the eyes. "Make haste in reply."

"You're not soldiers," Sailen answered.

"And how did you come to assume that?"

"You lack the upkeep and discipline.... I can tell from recent experience." Sailen turned to look at the man behind him. For the first time he noticed their faces were not of privileged men, and neither of them held their weapons in the proper regard his father had once shown him.

"Experience?" the injured man questioned. He began applying pressure to his hand, while rummaging through his package material for bandaging.

"A rank came upon my homestead two nights ago."

"Aye, and they have yet to return. Yet you, a boy nigh upon manhood, freely walk the Vefren path...." Milfor addressed Sailen.

"What's it to you Milfor? Captain of... two..." Sailen knew emotional antagonizing would put the men on edge.

"You speak boldly for one who's odds are currently against him." Though it was evident the men were not soldiers, their malice and unknown purpose made Sailen extremely uneasy. He was unsure of their intent and had no idea how to best them. At present, he'd rather them be soldiers and know he'd have to fight his way out. A gust of wind swept suddenly through the air. The aggressive breeze sent chills through the men, turning their excitement. Sudden darkness crept over the skies and storm clouds overshadowed the sun. The day turned into an eerie twilight, as if a storm were about to let loose on the

29

mountain. The men looked around, unaware.

"There's witchery about this region, I feel it," one of the soldiers said looking around.

"Shut up," Milfor commanded, with just as much uneasiness in his voice.

"Enough of this, you're coming with us boy. We're going to see what became of that Capital rank that fell upon your village."

The horses stirred uncontrollably, whining and prancing indiscreetly. A silent lightening cracked across the sky. Milfor jumped forward and grabbed Sailen, tossing his blade to the ground.

"Saddle up!" he commanded to the others as he forced Sailen towards his horse, reaching for his saddle bag. A second streak of lightening crossed the sky as the men mounted their horses. Sailen struggled against Milfor as he pulled rope from his saddle bag and attempted to bind his hands.

"You have no right!" he barked as his one hand slid from Milfor's headlock. He then proceeded to kick him in the back. His youthfulness proved to his advantage, as he was swifter than the older man. He turned to retrieve his blade and saw the elderly woman walking slowly off the Vefren path towards the group. Yuefil was of full figure; she was tall for of her age. Her stark white hair flowed freely past her shoulders. Her clothing was tattered, and she wore tan garments, save her leather boots. She carried a hilted mace on her side.

With fierce calm in her gaze, she approached the group. The two men facing Sailen were unaware of her presence, but Milfor charged foeward with his sword raised high, "Halfkin!" Turning to face Milfor, Sailen was struck in the face with the flat side of his sword.

Sailen's vision went black with the crack of his senses before he hit the ground. The pain lulled in and out with his consciousness. With the remnants of his senses he saw the three men, two on horseback, attacking Yuefil, and Meerah stumbling over the path from the direction of the camp. Losing complete consciousness, He collapsed on the ground.

Meerah locked eyes with Yuefil and was immediately frozen in place, unable to move. She stood at the edge of the Vefren path motionless as she watched the men move on her neighbor.

Withdrawing her mace, Yuefil made contact with Milfor's sword when he attempted to hack at her. "We shall make light work of this," she stated calmly.

Yuefil recovered, doubling her grip, and struck Milfor, splitting his head at the base of his skull before he could retract. His death was instant. Sidestepping his collapsing body, she readied for the other men approaching on horseback.

"Rid-em!" she said looking at the horses. Both animals bucked, viciously tossing the men in the air. With three strides Yuefil was upon them, crushing one's throat with a single blow. She ripped her weapon away, and turned the remaining man, now beckoning on his knees.

"Please! Please! Do not kill me! I bid thee no further harm!"

"Flee!" she screamed at the man. He stumbled to his feet, and took off up back up the Vefren path, glancing back only to ensure he wasn't being pursued. His wails drifted into the distance as he stammered away.

"Where are the others?" Yuefil asked Meerah as she walked toward Sailen. Meerah was completely bewildered by what she had just witnessed and didn't realize she had regained control over her body. Stumbling over the rock, she ran towards Sailen too. "No, you holster the horses, I will take care of him," Yuefil ordered. "What happened to the others?" she asked again, moving to pick up Sailen's unconscious body.

"Osem and Bell are a few yards off the path at a camp we set up through the night..." Meerah stepped over one of the corpses and was immediately reminded of the horror that befell them just a few nights ago. "My parents were killed during the attack on our homestead a few nights ago." And with her attention completely taken off the horses she turned back to Yuefil in anger. "Where were you?!" she demanded.

4 TALL TALES

Meerah and Yuefil brought the two horses back to the camp, one carrying an unconscious Sailen and the few useful items they'd taken from the men on the road. Meerah was steaming with anger and curiosity, waiting for Yuefil to account for her whereabouts the night their homestead was raided. But, Yuefil insisted on holding her story until Sailen woke. They left the dead men on the road, assuming anyone who stumbled upon them would attribute their deaths to the soldiers.

Bell woke to his unconscious son and the neighbor he assumed was dead, but he wasn't surprised. "You're alive and well," he gestured at Yuefil.

"Aye, as are you… for the most part."

Meerah was at odds with the exchange, but didn't know where to start her inquisition. Yuefil pulled Sailen down off the horse and laid him on the ground, wrapping her sheepskin sack to lay his head.

"Sailen, it's time to wake up."

"What happened?" Bell asked.

"He was attacked by three men on the road. They were on their way to scavenge what was left of the homestead, or so they thought. He held his ground pretty well, especially considering...." She looked at Bell and he nodded in return.

Sailen's eyes blinked and he bolted upright. Immense agony radiated through his head. He tried to jump to his feet, but was lightly restrained by Yuefil.

"Relax, you're ok," Bell said, looking at Yuefil with a smile.

Meerah felt relief overcome her seeing that he was still alive. She looked over to confirm her brother was still asleep then turned her attention back to the group.

"What happened?" Sailen asked groggily, "What happened to you?"

All eyes turned to Yuefil as she replied, "pack up, we must get to ORium by sunset, and I will tell all on the road."

"That's impossible." Bell replied.

"No questions, just move, we need to get back to the road."

Sailen adjusted himself as he stood up, shaken and embarrassed, hoping that Meerah didn't see him get knocked out from the blow. He shook off the embarrassing thought, realizing the urgency of their situation. The day was still, the sun high in the sky and the elements of the mountain at an odd peace, but the threat of their situation remained.

Meerah motioned toward Sailen to help her pack the armor onto one of the horses as they grudgingly followed

Yuefil's orders. The horse remained calm as they hurridley distributed the weight of the armor and equipment around its saddle. Yuefil picked up Osem, who remained asleep, to everyone's bewilderment, and placed him on the saddle of the other horse, strapping him in position.

Once they were ready they made for the road a short distance away. Sailen noticed Meerah was eyeing him, as if she was trying to tell him something, but he couldn't guess what it was. They crossed the wall opening up to the Vefren path and beheld the men Yuefil had just killed. Yuefil around the bodies, and led them up the road towards Orium. "Be on guard, these men may not be the only lurkers on the path."

The path was straight and the fairly easy to walk. Sailen was perplexed. Why was the path so laid out when his homestead and Elvanor Forest were the only places on this side of the mountain? Why was the path laid as if it were well traveled, when neither was of major consideration for inhabitants of Yeelerah? His questions were endless. The wolves? The soldiers? The men? Yuefil's disappearance?

Suddenly he began to remember the scene, and the fight that had left him unconscious when Yuefil broke the silence.

"As much as I know I will tell you, but first I shall let Bell bring forth truths unknown to the two of you."

Sailen and Meerah looked at Bell.

Then Sailen recalled aloud, "Yuefil's a halfkin?" She looked back with a wry smile, reflecting friendship and reassurance. Sailen and Meerah knew they did not need to fear her.

Bell showed no sign of surprise at Sailen's statement, continuing to guide his luggage-bearing horse over the short wall.

"Sailen and Meerah, as you know our families have been close all of your lives..." Bell began. "We've lived modestly and taught you both the basics of life, and little about the Hulrien King's empire in the known world. What you do not know is that Meerah's parents, Sailen's mother, and myself were once aristocrats of the Hulrien Empire."

The path began to veer upward. They were beginning to see signs of life in the mountain. The world apart from humanity still existed in its own balance. Wind began to pick up in the paths of the mountain, howling and swaying the brush. Yuefil continued to lead them confidently, as if she had been there before. "Rinah and Hittra, Meerah's parents, were decedents of wealth and served as the late Hulren King Tolnor's ambassadors in foreign affairs. Sailen's mother and myself were also nobles of the Royal Halfkin Court, advisors on foreign and domestic relations.

"At the turn of the last millennia, more than forty years ago, the Queen birthed a boy, then heir to and now king on the Hulren Throne. Three years into his life the boy did not show signs of being a descendent of the halfkins, as he should have. There were no signs or bursts of magic or unexplained events, as usually occurs when such children are birthed and haven't yet mastered their powers. Suspicions began to grow of the queen's potential infidelity, as she was a mortal woman that the king bound himself to.

"There are no limitations on halfkins, they can

choose whatever romantic fate they want and still produce such offspring, as many do. So in this case, the suspicions were surmounting amongst inner circles. By the time the boy had reached the fifth year of life, King Tolner began covering for him, in turn saving his dignity. He projected his powers through the boy, to give the illusion the boy was indeed halfkin and his own.

"On the child's sixth birthday, the last year of significance for halfkin, at which if no powers are evident there will be none, the king coerced a confession of infidelity from the queen. The child he'd grown to love was not his, but that of his queen and a mortal guard Bilthren. Forsaken with grief, the king spent two days agonizing over his decision. His delay in action enabled the queen to organize a plot for his assassination with a group who call themselves The Pro-Order."

"What is The Pro-Order?" Meerah asked.

"They are an anti-halfkin extremist group. During the era of the true king they were powerless, but now they seek out and oppress all supernatural beings, promoting hatemongering through fear and propaganda," Yuefil replied with battements. "Their influence today is insurmountable. They have succeeded by placing the false Hulren King on the throne."

"I don't understand, if the Hulren King isn't of halfkin linage, why was he allowed on the throne?" Sailen asked in confusion. He and Meerah didn't know much about the empire, but their lives were based off the assumption that the king was indeed the rightful king.

"Let me finish," Bell interjected. "As then, and until this day, only few knew Tolner's heir wasn't in fact his.

Once the king found out, he consulted a small council of halfkins, exactly seven including himself. Meerah's father and I were also there. "

Bell paused to give both Meerah and Sailen a moment to take in what he'd just shared with them. Holding up his hand to stop their questioning, he continued. "Each of us swore and oath of secrecy until the king had made a decision on what he'd do with his estranged wife and her child. But the queen acted faster than he did. Her malice had gone unnoticed through the years; none knew nor suspected the treachery she was capable of. We don't know the extent of which it was orchestrated or who was involved, but King Tolner was ambushed during his seclusion in the King's Tower. Lights flared and the clanging of steel could be heard through the castle from the towers peek. It was an open flat for surveying the kingdom. Several guards rushed to the tower, but before they could get there, nobles in the courtyard saw the king's body plunge from the tower into the falls, with a wooden stake protruding from his chest.

"When the guards arrived at the King's Tower, they found three of the kings' guards and a beheaded halfkin noble. The Queen Regent, she was named such after the king's death, counseled and convinced the empire aristocrats and dignitaries that the halfkin aristocrats organized a plot to assassinate the king and put a republic in place. One in which they'd all have equal rule.

"The Queen's theory was accepted as true because the only living witnesses to the king's death were the attending guards, who were later discovered to be Pro-Order, and a dead halfkin. Per law, the council waited five days to recover the king's body. It was never found thus they proceeded with blessing the Queen Regent's supreme power over the empire. To avoid suspicion, she maintained the balance of the empire, passed no new laws and didn't press the prosecution of halfkins living within the kingdom, aside from those nobles she wrapped in her conspiracy of the king's death plot. Many of us fled knowing our cause wouldn't be availed.

"Noble halfkins remaining in the capital made straight for Orium, and sent word to those on leave. One of them was your mother, Sailen. They were advised to leave as well. Of the original seven in the king's council, five of us made it out alive. Ilfern was the halfkin murdered by the Pro-Order and planted at the King's Tower the night of his murder. Another was captured in her attempt to flee.

Meerah's parents, Elogh, Yuefil and I made it to ORium safely under the guise of mortals. From there, we aimed to maintain our appearance, as our cause had no leverage to remove the queen and her child from the capital.

"Once the child came of age, the queen began to crusade the will of the Pro-Order, which was also her own. The young Hulren King, through the control and influence of his mother, used the conspiracy of the king's assassination to swear against and outlaw halfkins in the empire. He denounced his ability, which the select few knew never really existed, and used his powers as King to hunt and imprison halfkins within the empire.

"At the ten-year mark of the king's assassination, the community of noble halfkins living in Orium, seventeen in total, as some had rejoined us, solidified our mortal guise unprosecuted. Meerah's parents, Alily, Yuefil and I left ORium to build the homestead between Elvanor and the Vefren path, to get further from the influence of the empire and regain our means.

"Our cause only weakened with time, growing hopeless as the new King's power and influence grew. We came and went to Orium and various parts of the empire, witnessing the campaign to purge halfkins and other supernatural beings spread across the world. Our network weakened; we had no means to restore balance or reclaim the Hulren throne."

"What happened to my mother?" Sailen asked coming to a stop. Meerah paused and looked as well.

"Keep moving." Sailen looked around, noting the scenery wasn't changing much as Yuefil continued to guide them.

"About a year after you were born, your mother's resentment toward our situation grew aggressively. She became fixed on righting the wrongs of the world we lived in so that you could live in the grace we'd fallen from. Our contentment of living out our lives outside the path, hoping to escape the grasps of the Pro-Order oppression and destruction, changed with new life. Within that same year, Yuefil had returned from a four-year mission with a child just three years old. She was in Yelerah recruiting living halfkins to strengthen our network, but when Pluriep's magic began to appear, Yuefil had to flee the cities before they were discovered."

Sailen and Meerah looked at each other with surprise at Bell alluding to Pluriep being halfkin. "During her voyage back to our side of the Verfren Mountains,

Yuefil encountered a mystic who had escaped the queen's castle, where she was held captive for nearly a decade. In aiding Yuefil on her journey back, she shared news of royal halfkin descendants believed to be roaming in Elvanor. Once Yuefil returned, our arrangements allowed for your mother to set out and find the royals while we remained at the homestead. That was fourteen years ago."

There was silence as they continued forward. Sailen didn't know where to begin resolving his curiosities. Yuefil stopped abruptly, turning to the left where the mountain sloped downward into dark wooded area. The mountain was heavily wooded on both sides of the trail, but the direction of the Hflee Tunnels was exceptionally dark.

"Here we turn off the path, and take to the Hflee Tunnels, they will get us to Orium in a third of the time. These tunnels were constructed ages ago, and have been forgotten overtime. They are very dangerous. Many curiosities and mythic animals still dwell in the darkness of the Yelerah, and the Hflee Tunnels."

The sun was near the end of its ascension across the sky. Twilight was hours away and with Bell's tale finished, Sailen and Meerah were both brought back to reality, suddenly aware of their surroundings. The mountain was heavily wooded on both sides of the trail, but the direction of the Hflee Tunnels was exceptionally dark.

Their walk off the path proved to be more difficult than it appeared it would be. The trees on the mountain were broad at the center, and densely populated. Brush and shattered mountains stones scattered throughout the forest floor. The passages between the trees were narrow and jagged. Their balance and footing was continuously compromised on the uneven terrain. Sailen wondered what could cause so many pieces of the mountain to come loose. Several times they had to maneuver with the horses at angles to continue in their general direction.

Meerah walked swiftly to check on Osem in his saddle, to find he was still asleep.

"Why is he still sleeping?" She eyed Yuefil with suspension.

"Because I am keeping him that way," she responded. "It is best for all of us to make it to Orium with little distraction and delay as possible. I promise no harm has been done. You know me, I am the same neighbor and family you've grown up with. You will soon learn, our morality is only strengthened by our magic abilities."

"Soon learn?" Meerah asked.

"Were you not listening to Bell? We are all halfkins." Yuefil walked the horse over to Sailen and Meerah. "Our families decided to hide your powers to protect you from the empire, even in our seclusion. We suppressed each of your abilities from a young age, except Osem as he has not yet begun to display his magic abilities. It will take three halfkins to lift the bounds. But before we do so, it is paramount that you understand the risk of exposure within the bounds of the Hulren Empire is death." Yuefil turn and gestured for them to follow her off the path and into the woods.

Sailen now assumed his father knew a lot more than he let on. Meerah grabbed Sailen's hand after he escaped from sight behind a tree and brush. He looked back and gripped her hand tighter. They both began to feel the sense of adventure.

5 AN EVENTFUL NIGHT

An hour into their walk, the group came upon a hedge structure. Yuefil waited for the rest of the group to catch up, while tightening the straps holding Osem in place. They stood alongside a slope, where large stones laid upon one another against the exposed mountain rock. The structure stretched for several yards down the mountainside, trees spread further down the opening, heavy with greenery. Despite the abundant vegetation in the area there were no signs of life.

Breaking through the flat, Sailen and Meerah walked right up to the stones, admiring their magnificence. They'd never seen anything outside of their homestead before, and the massive structure was alluring. As he touched it, Sailen observed his surroundings and thought about the changing of his world with new optimism. All he had learned over the past several hours, though he had yet to truly take it in, was but a factor of the sense of living he was feeling. He was far from home, exploring the world beyond. He was indeed living a life apart from all that he'd known.

"A short way down there is a gap in the stones, and a doorway, for those who can see it. That is the entrance to the Hflee Tunnels. We must be careful. These tunnels are void of light, and contain sharp turns and sudden drops. Stay close, stay on the path, and keep the pace." Yuefil stated as she led the way down the path. The mountain's slope slowed their pace as they resisted the forward inertia hastening them along.

"Yuefil, you still haven't told us where you were…" Meerah was insistent on getting answers as the weight of her loss began to set in. She looked up at Yuefil guiding the horse carrying her younger brother. She wanted answers, she wanted to know why no one was there to help or save her parents, and why if they were indeed halfkin, did they not save themselves.

"I was backtracking the wolves from Elvanor," Yuefil responded. Anticipating her further questions, she continued. "I sensed their coming within hours and traveled to the edge of the forest before their arrival. Flanking their outer perimeter, I followed their trail back through the forest, assuming Bell and your parents were able to handle what was to come. I underestimated the situation, not knowing the soldiers were making their way to our homestead. I was mistaken and for that I am eternally sorry. I promise you the loss weighs on me heavier than you can imagine. And I thank you all for your parts in ensuring them a proper burial." Yuefil eyed Sailen with special gratitude. "Alas, the effort was not entirely in vein, because

I found them."

Bell caught Yuefil's attention immediately, "Found who?" he asked with impatience.

"Alily and the royals."

"What?" Bell's calmness encompassed his disbelief and excitement. "Well where is she? Why didn't she return with you?"

"They are prisoners of The Rixew, guarded by the Elvanor wood tribe, men and woman who worship the wolfs as deities. No harm has come to them, they are well fed and treated well, but they are imprisoned all the same. I came upon their camp, barely visible to the sentinels and crept my way to an unwatched cell. There I found Alily. She is in good health Bell, that I assure you. And as beautiful as the day she left." Bell let out a sigh of relief.

"Then we are going the wrong way, shouldn't we being going to free them?" Bell stopped walking.

"The effort would be futile, although tribe's people are mortals, there are many and the Rixew protect them with elemental magic."

Sailen and Meerah were unable to comprehend the rate at which lives were changing.

"I don't even know what either of you are talking about, true or not, or what we are doing here. None of this makes sense. And add to it you now tell me my mother is alive." Sailen's frustration was evident in his tone. "What are we to do, abandon her and go off into the empire to do what?"

"I agree with Saileen, what are we doing? Yuefil, you keep saying we need to get to Orium but why? What good is it for us to run to a city within the empire? It seems like there's no safe place for us."

Meerah halted. She and Sailen stared from Yuefil to Bell, waiting for more answers. They were now at the tunnel entrance, standing at a narrow gap in the stones. Cool air flowed out as if there was a breeze coming from within and the depth of its darkness seemed endless.

"The royals are being held captive until the Thesmian Faun passes judgment on their involvement in the death and betrayal of King Tolnor. The wolves will not aid the royals in reclaiming the empire, but they are bound to protect innocent halfkins, as is their will and the reason they were at our homestead the night the soldiers arrived."

"We must find the faun, before we are captured or killed, and for that we will need Elogh to help lift the bounds on you two," Yuefil said nodding toward them.

Without another word, Yuefil entered the mountain, leading the horse through the narrow doorway. Sailen followed. Passing the threshold, he immediately felt the rush of darkness come over him. It was the darkest night he'd ever witnessed, but the coolness of the air felt calm through the tunnels.

As his eyes adjusted to the darkness, he could feel Meerah and his father close behind. Vaguely making out the outline of the horse and then Yuefil, he slowly walked forward, feeling into the darkness to keep his balance. The horse's hooves made a light trotting noise on the stone floor, echoing through the cavern. Feeling Meerah's hand lightly gripping his shoulder, Sailen shifted his pack so she could get a full grasp as they continued forward in silence.

Sailen realized it'd been a while since they had eaten, and wondered if Yuefil would make them wait until they reached Orium. So much was happening so fast, he felt as if he were forgetting how to think. His mother was still alive, he had halfkin abilities, he was now on a quest to find a mythical faun, all while being hunted by the empire. This began to weigh in the back of his mind, as fatigue and hunger set in the front. He could tell Meerah was feeling the same as she dragged behind him.

They continued in the dark for what seemed like hours. Yuefil led them slowly along the stone path, which was perfectly laid out. There were slight breaks in the elevation, so every turn was navigated will caution. Three times Sailen thought he'd heard noises trailing behind them, but he assumed his imagination or tiredness was getting to him. The horse trots continued their silent echo.

Yuefil stopped abruptly, causing Sailen to stumble into her in his hypnotic stupor. Meerah was slower to react, bumping into Sailen and causing their bundles to clank loudly from the metal armor. Yuefil hushed them, and shot Bell a look to keep them in line.

"Ahead is a stone doorway that opens onto the edge of Orium. I believe it's night, so we must be quiet and swift. Elogh's house is not far from the opening so with luck we should have no trouble." As Yuefil continued forward, Sailen could see nothing but a dead end ahead. Confused, he looked at Meerah who had the same expression. He'd lost track of time and was not sure how many hours had passed.

"Do you hear that?" Meerah shook at Sailen's shoulder.

"Yes."

"Shh... keep close after Yuefil, we don't not have time

to idle," Bell instructed. Yuefil was at a stand still. She stepped to the side of the horse and began to study the stone for a brief moment. She lifted her right hand, and just as her palm touched the wall it slid up opening to the landscape outside of the mountain.

Night was upon Orium. The sky was clear and full of starlight. The mountainside sloped down to a view of the city, nearly a mile away. From their distance they could see the town was frantic with activity. There were small buildings and homes closely knit, comprising the city. In the center there was a large military structure, situated like a fort. It had three high pillars at each corner, twice the height of its triangular base. There was a mob at the town center around the building and more people coming out of their homes to join. Capital soldiers nearly outnumbered the town's people and were hostilely caroling them to the building.

"Something is not right, there are never this many soldiers from the capital here," Yuefil said, walking forward.

Bell pushed Meerah and Sailen forward. "Let's hurry before we're seen."

Sailen noticed his father cast a worried look into the darkness as they stepped out of the tunnel. Yuefil slowly took Osem from the pack horse, nudging the animal to the side.

"What about the armor and pack, we can't just leave the those?" Sailen eyed her.

"Yes we can, we don't need more than we can carry. And from the looks of it, money will not be easily found here tonight. Keep moving."

"Hurry, it's this way to Elogh's. Do not speak with anyone and stay close." Bell took the lead, walking swiftly toward the town. They were about a mile from the city's edge. As they approached the first tenement, the noise of the crowd was filled with anguish and shouting soldiers. From the commotion, it appeared that there was city a registration going on by order of the empire. The soldiers were making sure all citizens were present to do so. Luckily, Bell was leading the way through the crowd, so they did not draw any unnecessary attention to themselves.

As they passed several people, Sailen couldn't help but notice the inquisitive looks they were receiving. People seemed to know they didn't belong. Most of the crowd was groaning rampart remarks of wanting to hurry back to their homes.

"This way." Bell made a left down a street lined with single homes.

There was no one on the street, which caused him to grow nervous. Sailen was only a few steps behind his father as they walked up to one of the single homes. Bell walked along the side of the house in a narrow gap to the rear. Sailen looked to make sure Meerah and Yuefil were close behind. The alley was tight and the adjacent houses were nearly touching each other. When they reached the back, there was a garden with and single chair and table. Above the entrance hung an unlit lantern. Bell approached the door and knocked three times, then turned to confirm they were all there. A man opened the door. Nearly seven feet tall, broad and muscular, Elogh Kilont stood in the doorway.

"Rest assured, you show up on registration day, you old goat," Elogh pulled Bell in for a tight embrace. "It's been too long old friend." As he let him go, he looked upon the rest of the group."Yuefil! Oh come in all of you, quick hurry." Ushering them through the door, he eased it shut and slid a lock block in place.

The home was a single room. There was a coal oven, eating table, and carpet laid out covering most of the floor space. Near the front door was a single bed and nightstand. The room was lit with four lanterns placed in each corner of the home.

"I take it the soldiers that marched through here to made it to your homestead…" Elogh began.

"Yes, but many did not make it out," Yuefil quickly responded.

"You two old coots still got fight in you, huh." Elogh smiled.

He walked toward a cabinet and began pulling out bread and an assortment of cheese and jam fixings. He motioned for everyone to join him at the table and passed around the food. Sailen and Meerah sat down to eat immediately. Osem began to stir and reached out for Meerah. She sat him on her lap and split food between the two of them.

"Not exactly… The Rixew did most of the work, with the exception of the few whom Sailen was able to fend off." Yuefil shot Sailen a proud smile.

"Sailen ehh… you must take after your mother. A sage and a warrior if there ever was such a combination. No offense Bell. But the Rixew you, say? The soldiers must have lured them out of Elavanor?"

"I believe this to be true. Elogh there are many things happening which we do not have the time to talk through. Bell and I need you to help lift the bounds we've placed on

Sailen and Meerah so they can access their magic."

"Why?" Elogh began to question. "I will hold my questions until this is done. Shall we proceed now?"

"Yes, and as we do you should also know that Alily located the royals in Elavanor."

"What?! This cannot be..."

"We must move quickly, we can talk more later, but with the town in registry, we must do the task while the three of us are all here."

Yuefil took a large bite of bread and cheese and got up from her chair. She motioned for Bell to join her next to Elogh.

"Meerah, please sit Osem in the seat." Meerah moved Osem to the chair, handing him a piece of bread to nibble on. Though awake, he was still a bit drowsy.

"Both need to be aware that your magic is connected to your inner will, it is a muscle that needs to be paired with thought to be used. You must, above all, master it with discipline and control over not only it but your thoughts too. Calmness is true strength, mastery is full power." Sailen felt anxiousness building within him and his stomach knotting with nausea.

The responsibility weighed on him more than the excitement. "Wait, this seems to be too dangerous. I am not ready. Three days ago I was a farm boy, now you tell me all this and that my heritage is more than I know. This is madness." He stood up and took a step away from everyone. "Dad this can't be real, I am not halfkin, I've never felt anything magical in my life, and if so, why would you let me grow up in such ignorance?"

"We don't have time for this Sailen," said Yuefil.

"I know you're afraid son." Bell interrupted. And I know this is a lot to take in, but life is never simple even when it's what you want most. Three days ago you were a farm boy, yes, but you had dreams of living beyond that, and now that opportunity, that reality is here. It's ok to be nervous but don't let fear overcome you. Fear is not in you; you are halfkin." Bell held his son's shoulder and looked at Meerah, who began to cry. "Your mom was against us placing the bounds on you, as was Alily, but ultimately we thought it was for the best. You both know the thrill of adventure and youthful arrogance because of the bounds. Magic would have led you astray before you were ready in our seclusion. The circumstances are unfortunate, but at this point you can accept them or run from your awakening."

Meerah stood up from her chair and walked over to Sailen. Grabbing his hand, she gave him confidence and the strength of eternal friendship.

"We're ready." Sailen said.

Elogh, Bell, and Yuefil, formed a circle around Meerah and Sailen. They began to focus intently on the two of them, not saying a word and not giving insight into what they were thinking. Sailen observed each of them and began to wonder if this was all a joke. With their eyes closed, their trance-like state exuded immense focuse. Sailen and Meerah waited for some outburst of enchantment or motion, but nothing happened.

Sailen turned toward Meerah and cracked a smile, hoping she was as amused as he was. When she turned to him he felt a sharp pain in his chest, as if something inside it being was convulsing. Together they grasped their chests.

Sailen doubled over, sprawling onto the floor. The three moved in closer without saying a word or breaking their focus. The pain increased in intensity as Sailen forced himself across the floor, letting out a loud sigh, then an instant it vanished.

"All done. Eat while we have time." Bell stated nonchalantly, walking toward the table.

"It's like uncramping a muscle." Elogh smiled.

Sailen reached over to help Meerah to her feet, but was surprised to see she was already standing. Hurrying to his feet, he walked back to eat, still feeling nauseous. "I don't feel any different," Meerah said looking at Yuefil.

"Well, it would be nice if this bread were toasted; easier to spread jam," Yuefil said seeming to ignore her notion. "Why don't you heat this up, add a little tinge to this for me." She pushed the bread over to Meerah, who looked at Sailen bewildered.

He looked at the bread, thinking to himself of how one could will bread to toast. "Will doesn't work that way. it has to be applied physically for something to happen, fire is physical not imaginative," He said out loud.

"Is that what you believe?" Elogh replied. Sailen turned to Elogh, he had heard stories of this man many times throughout his life. He was impressed with the idea of him from his father's stories. And to Sailen, his previous level of admiration did not do Elogh justice. He was a massive presence, but almost gentle in nature. Embarrassed by his response, Sailen turned back to the bread. Suddenly it burst into bright orange flames, rocketing to the ceiling.

Sailen's eyes widened with disbelief as the flames grew uncontrollably, Bell ran to the sink to fill a bucket with water as the fire began to catch the rest of the table. He threw what water filled the bucket on the flaming table to no avail. Yuefil and Elogh appeared to be conjuring water out of thin air, but smoke was filling the house quickly. Sailen and Meerah huddled around Osem trying to avoid the flames and fume.

"Put it out!" Meerah screemed.

"I can't!" Yuefil replied looking at Elogh.

"Neither can I. Meerah did you feel a magic surge when you started the fire?"

"No I didn't feel anything. I didn't do that." She struggled to hold Osem in her arms, as he played wild with joy.

They all turned to Sailen.

"It wasn't me" he said.

"Out of the house!" Bell screamed.

Elogh ran to his nightstand and pulled out a sack. He moved around the house picking up random valuables. "Back door," he said.

Sailen helped Bell grab their packs and get Meerah to the door with Osem.

On his last look inside the house, Sailen saw flames catch the ceiling. He stumbled into the back alley, rushing behind Yuefil, Elogh and Meerah making their way to the street.

"What happened?" Sailen asked looking to the others for answers.

"I think Osem discovered his magic," Bell smiled. Suddenly Sailen understood why none of them could stop the fire. He'd heard of how in the first year of a halfkin child discovering their magic, only someone directly related by blood could overcome or help tame their magic when it was loose.

"I'm afraid Elogh is going to lose his home." Sailen said.

"He won't be the only one; that fire will spread until there is nothing else to catch. Assuming Meerah doesn't tap into her powers tonight."

Smiling to himself, Sailen suddenly was filled with belief. When they caught up to Elogh and the others, they were huddled behind a house just outside the square.

"The town's people will be aware of the fire at any moment now." Elogh said survey the street. "What is the plan?"

Bell looked around frantic. "We should go back into the Heflee Tunnels for the night; wait this out until dawn. The town will know you have gone Elogh, the time for you covert alias is over. The next phase of our mission is laid before us. We must seek out the Thesmian Faun."

Sailen turned around to see smoke rising from the house toward the night sky. Flames stretched across the roofline two rows of houses back. In that instant, a bell began to toll in the corner of the neighborhood. Shouts rose from various areas of the homes. People emerged from the alleys to witness the fire. No one seemed to have noticed their group as they rushed to watch the sprading fire.

"Fine. Let's go now," Elogh responded.,He turned to Yuefil to lead the way. She moved hurridly, leading them across the crowd and into the streets heading away from the commotion. People bumped and shoved as they went. Once they made it to the nearest opening, they could see a group of soldiers beckoning the townspeople, trying to restore order. Sneaking past, they ducked into the nearest alley and made their way back to the edge of Orium.

As they made it out of the city, Meerah turned suddenly. The flames were rising above the roofs from the short distance; and shouts could be heard vocalizing the panic and mayhem.

"We can't leave that fire burning, many people will lose their homes. Yuefil you must tell me how to put this out." Meerah looked filled with guilt. Being the only one who could subdue Osems magic, she had to do something.

Bell approached Meerah; placing his hands on her shoulders he began to instruct her. "You have to still your mind. Will your magic. It's a muscle, feel your will and control it."

Sailen felt his own nerves began to calm as he observed. Meerah looked with intent into the distance. Moments passed slowly. She focused to try and control her breaths, and felt a calm come over her. Sailen observed her patiently. Soon the flames began to lessen. He could see them falling below the roofline. The fire was smoldering out.

"I did it!" Meerah turned to Bell with a cheerful smile.

"You did," Bell responded.

"Without air, fire can't breathe, I focused on separating the two. I willed it, and it worked!" Meerah threw her arms around Bell, relieved.

"I reckon it only spread to two other homes. The neighbors will be ok." Elogh said with a laugh, indicating he didn't really care for his neighbors.

"What are we going to do with you, little one?" Meerah said, taking Osem from Yuefil.

"We need to get going." Sailen said as he pointed to the left of the landscape. Over two dozen aromored men were in marching formation, facing their exact direction. "I think those soldiers are heading this way."

6 EARNED RESOLVE

The group shifted their focus from the troupe of soldiers organizing between the houses to executing their escape. But, Sailen could see the soldiers were now headed directly for them. "Follow me!" Yuefil grabbed Osem back from Meerah, and began to run up the mountain.

It was steep terrain. Soon after they began their sprint, Sailen could hear orders being screamed from the soldiers below. Looking over his shoulder, he could see they were in full pursuit. "They are coming!"

"Keep running!" Elogh screamed.

A number of soldiers dropped back and strung up arrows that were soon whistling through the air.

"They're firing!" Bell screamed to alert the others.

Arrows showered from the sky, barely missing them. They ducked and zigzagged, running up the mountain. Bell stopped to face the soldiers. Turning in his tracks, he focused on a set of soldiers close to him. With his magic, he sent them fflying through the air, down the mountainside. Holding Osem with one arm, Yuefil motioned toward the sky with her free hand. Grey clouds circled above and were followed by a fury of lightning strikes. Several soldiers were hit and instantly set ablaze in their armor, flailing to the ground screaming.

A full storm brewed in the sky. As they rushed closer to the tunnels, an arrow shot Bell through the back. Another pierced his leg, dropping him to the ground.

"Father!" Sailen screamed, running to his aid. Blood quickly stained Bell's tunic, as Sailen began to hoist him up. Unable to support his father's dead weight, they both dropped to the ground. Elogh rushed over to survey Bell's wounds.

"We have to get him into the tunnel."

"Go! Go without me, I am spent." Bell choked, blood spitting out of his mouth.

"No we are not leaving you," Sailen replied.

"I can't keep these soldiers from attacking us, we are going to lose here. That means capture and death. We must move." As Elogh lifted Bell up, a blade cut his backside. Sailen felt a tug on his shirt. He was thrust backward to the ground, and a group of soldiers were upon them.

As he scrambled to collect himself, he received a hard kick to his face. His vision blurred and his mouth filled with blood. Soon, he was forced to the ground by what he could only sense in his daze, was a very large soldier.

One soldier was joined by anothe and they continued kicking and beating Sailen's body. He could hear the same happening to his father and Elogh close by. They were quickly overwhelmed, blinded by pain and unable to recover themselves.

Fumbling to block the blows and get to his feet, Sailen mustered all his strength. Calming his mind against the pain and fury. He focused to clear his mind, elevating his senses above his agony, and thinking only of blazing fire. He felt magic exploding within him. Jets of flames erupted from the ground, encircling the three of them. Sailen could see Meerah and Yuefil up a short distance at the doorway of the tunnels. The fire circle separated them from the soldiers, who were regrouping around it.

Sailen crawled to his father. His shirt was covered in blood. Shaking Bell for a response, Sailen felt a sudden heaviness grow within hisself. His father's body was stiff and cold. It was lifeless. He turned him over, and Bell's eyes stared blankly up at Sailen, looking right through him. Tears flowed from Sailen's eyes. Before he could a think clear thought, Elogh grabbed him by the back of his shirt and dragged him toward the tunnel.

"Your father will understand." Elogh stated with a heavy voice. Sailen screamed in protest as Elogh pulled him effortlessly, watching as the flames moved closer and closer, and then consumed Bell's body on the earth.

"No!" Sailen broke Elogh's grip in a fit of rage and made toward the soldiers. He fixed his mind to shoot fire, throw rocks and assault the soldiers directly in his line of sight in every way imaginable, but to no avail. Once he was closer to their ranks, he picked up the sword of a fallen soldier. As he mad to attach the nearest man he was lifted and pulled through the air.

Landing on his back he looked up to see Yuefil

standing over him. "Getting yourself killed is not the best way to honor your father."

"If I take them with me it does."

"Oh now you're a warrior." She said snarkly. "Even with magic we cannot overcome their numbers for long. You have to be smarter."

Sailen looked at her shameful, but his rage was still blazing. Tears ran down his face from the heartbreak of losing his father. He didn't care who saw, or what happened to him as long as he could get revenge. He got to his feet and realized they were at the opening of the tunnel. Arrows continued flying through the air as the soldiers advanced up the mountain. Sailen assumed Yuefil or Elogh were misdirecting them so no one was hit. The soldiers were just a few yards away in numbers that could no longer be counted. Now was their only time to escape.

"Follow me." Elogh said as he went into the tunnel opening.

Meerah and Yuefil followed immediately. When Sailen moved to the entrance, Meerah backed out and bumped into him.

"Meerah, what are you doing?" Sailen asked. Before Meerah could respond, Osem began to clap and giggle out loud. Yuefil and Elogh now backed out of the tunnel as well.

"What's going on?" Sailed asked as they stumbled over each other.

From the darkness of the tunnel opening, he could see the set of silver eyes; snarls and glistening white fangs followed.

"Quiet" Yuefil whispered. "Clear the way, slowly."

They all backed out onto the open plane, and could hear the soldiers now making demands for them to surrender.

But the Rixew moved slowly out into the opening, in full view for all to see. Sailen was more impressed by the wolf than he could remember. The Rixew held a fierce, determined posture. And as he cleared the entrance, the group could hear the growing growls of his accompanying pack. They could only guess their numbers.

"What's the plan Yuefil?" Elogh asked nervously. There were now dozens of wolves coming out of the tunnel entrance. When Sailen looked back there was a regiment of soldiers braced for combay directly behind them. He gave their situation a few moments thought.

"We turn around, and see if they fight with us," Sailen replied. The blade he picked up was still in his hand. He turned to look The Rixew in his eyes and thought back to their last encounter, where the wolves saved his life. The lead wolf was again standing tall as his pack frenzied behind him. They locked eyes and Sailen felt a force like courage pass over him. Gripping the sword, he turned to face the army before them. Elogh and Yuefil moved in front of him.

A captain moved forward from the troupe. He was only a foot taller than Sailen, but harded in the face. "You are ordered to surrender to the empire, and will be taken to the capital for inquisition! On your knees for arrest, or we will take you by force alive or dead!" he paused. "And we will slay every one of those beasts in the waking."

Sailen's anger swelled. His father was dead. Nameless soldiers were after them without regard to reason, simply following orders from a king. In the moment he silently vowed he would come to see those who ruled and hunted him from a distance. Sailen's revenge would be finding the answers. He didn't care about being halfkin, he didn't care about justice for the royals, he just wanted justice for what was taken from him and Meerah. And he would have it.

Peace passed through him. He could sense all of his surroundings; the wolves heavy breathing, tense to the nape and ready for the taste of blood, Yuefil and Elogh ready for whatever was to come next, and the soldiers who stood brute and witless.

"I'm ready," Sailen said.

"Us too," Meerah answered, gripping Osem tighter.

Yuefil looked at them. "Your parents would be beyond proud, but you and Osem stay back and attack with magic only if you can. You must protect sure Osem I am sure he will naturally assist as well." Yuefil gave her a stern smile, and turned around. She drew her sword from her sheath, and was off. Elogh was right behind her, step-for-step. They charged in unison, with a radiating Sailen close behind.

.

7 DECISIVE ACTION

The wolves stampeded past the three halfkins racing down the mountainside. Sailen, felt the rush as he was surrounded. Energy seemed to flow into him, giving him strength and resolve. Sailen was only a few steps behind Yuefil and Elogh when they reached the soldiers and the bloodshed had already ensued. He came upon a soldier just his height and they locked swords aggressively. They exchanged blows back back and forth. He felt confidence holding his own. He out maneuvered and disarmed the man with a s single stike, forcing him to surrender. Grabbing him by his neck, Sailen thrust his face into the ground, holding him down with the heel of his boot. Looking up, he saw the wolves were holding nothing back. The killed anyone in their path, and had minimal losses on their side. Many of the soldiers began to retreat, within moments of the fighting.

"They're giving up," Elogh said looking toward

Sailen.

"This doesn't make any sense." Sailen observed the chaos and hesistated to let up the soldier that struggled beneath him.

"Elogh, follow and find out who their command is." Yuefil screamed, as she made her way toward Sailen.

Sailen said looked back up the mountain, but Meerah and Osem were nowhere in sight.

"Where's Meerah?!" He screamed. "Yuefil, where is Meerah?!" The soldier he was holding was nearly free from his restraint. Sailen turned him loose, then struck him directly in the head with his blade, knocking him out. He frantically surveyed the mountain, hoping to spot Meerah and Osem somewhere amongst the wolves.

"Bring him," Yuefil said heading towards the top of the mountain. Sailen grabbed the unconscious soldier and dragged him behind Yuefil. They arrived at the spot where they left Meerah and Osem. Wolves were returning as well to the area as well. Sailen tried to maintain a calm state, not to give away any appearance anxiousness or fear to the beasts.

"Soldiers came up here." She said as she pointed to sets of footprints that ran up the mountainside.

"There's no blood. Maybe they too them?" Sailen dragged the soldier flat on his back, removing his helm. He began striking him in the face with his fist. The man screamed as he regained consciousness,

"Stop! Stop!" Shakily, throwing his arms up. Blotching his face with his hands, he saw blood poured freely from several cuts. He propped himself up to see he was now trapped by to the two halfkins and a pack of monsotorous wolves. "Just kill me and get it over with," he screamed.

"No. Tell us what your rank was doing in Orium," Yuefil asked without hesitation.

"This is my regular station, I do not know anything of what else was going on," he stated plainly.

"Then speak of the rumors." She quickly retorted.

He sniffled, choking on his blood. "Soldiers came from the capital to facilitate a registration. That's all I know."

"And the ones who passed through Vefren Mountains?" Yuefil asked, now standing directly over him. "The wolves will not give you a quick death if we leave you to them."

"They were sent to destroy the homestead and then move onto Elevanor. I swear this is all I know! Please, please!"

"They've taken Meerah and the boy," Elogh came up through the pack of wolves. "They're taking them back to the capitol."

"We have to go after them," Sailen replied.

"Do you know why?" Yuefil asked Elogh.

"No, but I saw a rank of them rushing out of the city. I tried to pursue, but was taken by five soldiers. I managed to kill four of them and question the last. When they came upon your homestead it was in search of Meerah."

"What? Why Meerah?" Sailen was now completely lost on this new piece of information. "We must go after them!"

"Yes, but not in the manner you intend," Yuefil

answered.

"Have you ever even been to the capitol, boy? You will stick out like a thorn and for sure be thrown in the dungeon." The soldier laughed, giving his input. Sailen drew his sword directly on him.

"Sailen stop." Elogh grabbed him. "He taunts you for a quick death."

"Then I shall give it to him, and then we shall track down the troupe of soldiers before they make it to the capital, to rescure Meerah and Osem."

"Sailen calm yourself!" Yuefil turned to him. "Your anger is drop of water in a well of emotions you must learn to master. You must learn to control yourself or bring upon your own ruin before you accomplish any form of vengeance."

They stood in silence. For the first time Sailen noticed The Rixew at the forefront of the wolves. His eyes locked upon Sailen.

"You are proving your ability Sailen, but remember you are just a boy thrust into new world of responsibility and tragedy in the most unforeseen way. We must tread carefully if we wish to succeed."

"Succeed at what? Getting my dad killed, saving Meerah and Osem, or freeing the royals?" he asked in a bitter tone.

"So it is true then!?" The soldier said out loud before he could catch himself.

"What is your name boy?" Elogh pressed him.

"I thought you knew nothing?" Yuefil asked.

"I don't. My name is Eron. As you said, I only heard rumors."

"Rumors of royals?"

"Royals in Elavanor. Yes, I told you. I thought the soldiers were sent to destroy your homestead and then head to Elavanor. For what I knew not."

"Yuefil, we are wasting time. We must go after Meerah," Sailen jumped in. "Not to mention..." He motioned at the wolves standing among them. They were silent for a while.

"We must do both. The soldiers did not take Meerah on trivial hunch. As you stated Elogh, she was the target. We must find out why, just as we must save her. However, we cannot take on the Hulrien empire alone, even with what Halfkin resistance may remain inside the capitol."

"I will go after the girl," Elogh started. "You already know where the Royals are being held. Find the Thesmian Faun and take him there. I believe that is why the wolves are here."

"I think you're right," Yuefil agreed.

"And what about me. I'm going with Elogh," Sailen added.

"No, Eron will accompany me. If he values his life."

"What?" The soldier fumbled to his feet.

Ignoring the inquiry, Elogh continued, "you go with Yuefil. These wolves will guide you to the faun."

"Why me?"

"Because of your awakening," Yuefil began. "It connects you with them."

"What?"

"I'll explain later. As you so stated, there is no time to waste."

Sailen's nearly erupted in anger, but understood her point and calmed himself. "Elogh, we will meet you at Buckshed Market, outside the capitol in a fortnight."

"If I'm not there, I am either dead or imprisoned."

"And if we are not, we have been delayed."

"Understood," Elogh pointed to the soldier. "Take that armor off boy, you're with me... or I will slit your throat and leave you here." The soldier begrudgingnly shed his his armor.

"To the Heflee tunnels. The wolves will follow, then lead"   Yuefil motioned to Sailen.

Sailen looked at the Rixew, who was now a few steps closer to him. Much of the aggression had left, but he still projected immense power and fearsomeness. Sailen followed Yuefil to the tunnels. Looking back he saw Elogh pushing the soldier towards the city. The scene was now quiet and serene. He didn't like leaving Meerah's fate in the hands of a man he'd just met, but somehow he knew Elogh would find them. He entered the tunnels again. This time, he knew what the sounds were trailing behind him.

8 ELVANOR

Sailen was prepared for the darkness. It wasn't as frightening as the first time. The wolves led them through the tunnels, silent and focused. Sailen followed almost thoughtlessly with Yuefil by his side. The incline was drastically steeper headed downhill than he remembered, but he kept his thoughts to himself. The Rixew walked slowly in front of him, glancing back occasionally to meet his eyes. The constant watchfulness made him feel like a monitored child.

He thought much about the events that passed, and as soon as he had Yuefil alone he'd demand answers in the same way Meerah did. Why had he not stayed with her? Would he be alive if he did? Why did the King want her? It was all too much to think about. Mourning his father was delayed until these free moments of thought. e fought back the tears as best he could. The pain was unbearable, and the uncertainty of what was to come was frightening. Where were these wolves taking them? Was his mother really alive? He tripped over the uneven ground, catching himself before he fell.

"Careful," Yuefil whispered. "Not far now. This path isn't the same as the one we'd previously taken. I believe this path will bring us out directly to Elvanor."

Sailen didn't reply. He couldn't help but feel anger toward Yuefil. The deceit she and his father displayed incensed him in ways he could not easily dismiss. He was unsure of who he was, of what was next.

The Rixew began to slow in front of him. When they came upon the wolves stopped in front of a stonewall, they parted allowing the lead wolf to walk through. Sliding his muzzle from the bottom to the top of the wall, The Rixew eased open an unseen door. Light flooded the tunnel.

Sailen could taste the natural air rousing his senses. The freshness dulled the aches in his body. He walked slowly to the entrance, amazed at the forest spread before him. The trees stretched the sky and the sunlight danced between the greenery. The light gave the landscape a golden hue. Birds sang from their hidden nooks in various melodies. Sailen rubbed his eyes to clear his vision, unable to believe what he was seeing. The forest was vivid and alive. It was more vibrant than he could have ever imagined observing it from the distance of his homestead. For the briefest of moments, he saw a bird sized woman fly across his field of view.

"A fairy?" he whispered.

Just as he went to look for what he saw, a wolf lightly nudged him forward.

"Welcome to Elvanor." Yuefil proceed in front of

him. "Now let's find that faun."

To be continued…

PRESENT THOUGHT

We never know what will become in the end. All we know is the present and our perception of the past. In the end, all that matters is the present, as it is such, and what we take in the moment; what we make of each breath, what actions we choose, and what forces compel us. Eventually the present passes. Reminisce and fantasize, but move onwards to another future. 'Til the future is the present and the present is the end

Rixew Awakening

Q. Rosario

CPSIA information can be obtained
at www.ICGtesting.com
Printed in the USA
BVOW09*0527071117
499688BV00005B/17/P